The Elmwood Echoes

S. JIRILIN BABU

NOTION PRESS

India

Published by Notion Press 2025

Contents

"Friendship is the invisible thread that binds hearts together, creating echoes that linger long after the moments have passed. In the halls of Elmwood, these bonds became the foundation of a lifetime"

\- *S. Jirilin*

Foreword

The **Elmwood Echoes** follows John, Sam, and Ben through their college years at Elmwood Hall. Jirilin's poignant tale explores the power of friendship, self-discovery, and the challenges of growing up. As the trio faces life's ups and downs, their bond deepens, offering strength and resilience.

Each year in the story represents not just an academic milestone, but a personal one – an evolution of character, ambition, and identity. From the uncertainty and excitement of freshman year to the bittersweet farewells of senior year, the narrative captures the essence of youth, filled with moments of joy, pain, and profound realization.

What makes **The Elmwood Echoes** truly special is its universal resonance. The struggles and triumphs of John, Sam and Ben mirror our won experiences, whether it's facing personal loss, chasing after passions, or learning the true meaning of friendship.

This book is a testament to the enduring impact of college years – an era of discovery, of mistakes, of laughter, and of growth. Through *The Elmwood Echoes*, Jirilin gives us a story that linger long after the last page is turned, echoing the lessons learned and the friendships that remain.

Dr. L. Jabasheela,
Professor & Head,
Department of Computer Science and Engineering,
Panimalar Engineering College.

Foreword

College life is often regarded as one of the most transformative stages in a person's life - a vibrant tapestry of experiences, aspirations, and growth. **The Elmwood Echoes** brings this journey to life with unparalleled authenticity. It explores the foundations laid during freshman year, the strengthening of bonds through shared chaos, the trials and triumphs that mark the middle years, and the reflective moments of senior year as students prepare to step beyond the familiar brick walls.

Through chapters like "Brick by Brick," "Discordant Notes," and "Graduation Echoes," this book delves deep into the laughter resonating through dorms, the late-night study marathons, and the invaluable lessons learned both within and beyond classrooms. These pages capture the joy of friendships, the challenge of academic and emotional hurdles, and the enduring echoes of memories that follow students into the broader journey of life.

As you immerse yourself in the lives of John, Sam, and Ben, either relive your cherished memories or glimpse the adventures that lie ahead. May this foreword inspire you to treasure every challenge and joy in this remarkable chapter of life.

Dr. S. Suma Christal Mary,
Professor & Head,
Department of Information Technology,
Panimalar Institute of Technology.

Foreword

The book takes readers down memory lane, capturing the transformative unforgettable journey of three college friends. Each brings unique dreams and perspectives, forging a deep bond through shared triumphs and struggles. Together, they navigate exams, late-night talks, heartbreaks, and self-discovery, embodying the essence of college life.

As you dive into their world, you'll be transported to a time of growth, challenge, and unshakable bonds. For all its stress and uncertainty, college is a time when friendships are forged that can last a lifetime - when the mundane becomes memorable and the ordinary turns extraordinary. Through laughter, tears, and everything in between, these three friends show you the depth of connection that only comes when we're brave enough to be ourselves, and to let others do the same.

This story isn't just about classes and grades. It's about finding who truly you are, what you truly value, and how you navigate the complexity of relationships in a world that feels like it's changing faster than you can keep up. It's a testament to the power of friendship, resilience, and the uncharted roads we all must walk as we step into adulthood.

Jirlin, who values friendship and cherishes it, has connected the characters in such a very realistic way that you will be able to see yourself in these characters.

Mrs. S. V. Sreeja,
Vice Pricipal,
NVKS Vidyalaya.

Preface

Life is a symphony of moments - some harmonious, others discordant - but each note contributes to the melody of who we are. **The Elmwood Echoes** is a tapestry of those moments, set against the backdrop of Elmwood Hall, where friendships are forged, identities are discovered, and lives are forever changed.

This book is a reflection of the trials and triumphs that accompany the transition into adulthood. From the chaotic energy of dorm life to the quiet epiphanies of late-night conversations, it captures the raw, unfiltered journey of three friends navigating their college years. Together, they face personal struggles, academic pressures, and the ever-present question of purpose, weaving their individual stories into a shared legacy.

In these pages, you'll meet John, Sam, and Ben - each a unique star in their constellation, shining brightly yet uniquely. Through their laughter, tears, and moments of profound connection, *The Elmwood Echoes* explores the enduring impact of friendship and the echoes it leaves in our hearts long after the final chapter is written.

This story is for anyone who has ever found comfort in chaos, sought light in darkness, or discovered their voice amidst the cacophony of life. Welcome to Elmwood, where echoes of the past inspire the present and the future waits.

S. Jirilin Babu

Acknowledgments

Creating **The Elmwood Echoes** has been a deeply personal and transformative journey, made possible by the unwavering support of many remarkable individuals.

First and foremost, I am profoundly grateful to my father, **Dr. R. Suresh Babu Rajan**, whose wisdom, guidance, and love have been a constant source of inspiration. To my parents and family members, your belief in me has been the foundation of my strength.

Heartfelt thanks to the individuals who provided the forewords for this book: **Dr. L. Jabasheela**, **Dr. S. Suma Christal Mary**, and **Mrs. S. V. Sreeja**. Your words have added depth and credibility to this work, and I am deeply honored by your contributions.

To my dear friend **A. Aldo Ruban**, thank you for standing by me through every step of this journey. Your support has meant more to me than words can express.

Lastly, to my colleagues, thank you for your camaraderie, encouragement, and belief in my vision. You have all played a part in bringing this book to life.

This book is a reflection of the lessons learned and the memories cherished, and it stands as a testament to the impact of every person who has been a part of this journey. Thank you for helping me brings **The Elmwood Echoes** to fruition.

With gratitude,
S. Jirilin Babu

Prologue

Elmwood Hall stood as a silent witness to the stories it had cradled over the years. Its ivy-clad walls, weathered by time, bore echoes of laughter, whispers of late-night confessions, and the lingering warmth of countless friendships. For decades, it had been a haven for dreamers and seekers, a place where the young came to find their purpose and left with the imprints of unforgettable memories.

This is the story of John, Sam, and Ben - three individuals whose lives intertwined within Elmwood's hallowed halls. Each arrived with their own dreams and doubts, each carrying the weight of their past and the hope of their future. Together, they navigated the labyrinth of college life, forging a bond that would not only define their years at Elmwood but echo long after they had parted ways.

In these pages, we journey through their trials and triumphs, their moments of joy and heartache. From the chaos of freshman dorm life to the bittersweet farewells of graduation, their story is a testament to the resilience of the human spirit and the enduring power of friendship.

As the echoes of their time at Elmwood fade into the distance, they remind us that some places and people leave a mark that time can never erase.

Freshman Year

Building the Foundation

Brick by Brick

Introduces the setting – Elmwood Hall and establishes the beginning of John's college journey

John stood at the foot of Elmwood Hall, its towering spires casting long shadows across the cobblestone pathways. The building was a mix of old-world charm and modern functionality, a perfect representation of the college's rich history and its commitment to shaping the future. The ivy that crept up its walls seemed to whisper stories of generations past, of students who had walked the same paths, each leaving their mark on the institution.

Elmwood Hall was more than just a building; it was the heart of the college, a place where ideas were born, challenged, and refined. The hall's grand architecture with its gothic arches and intricate stonework was imposing and inviting, a sanctuary for learning and a fortress of knowledge. Inside, the hallways echoed with the footsteps of students, professors, and staff, each one a part of the college's living history.

For John, Elmwood Hall represented the beginning of a new chapter in his life. Standing there, with his suitcase in hand and a mix of excitement and nervousness in his heart, he could feel the weight of the journey ahead. This was the start of his college experience, a journey that would shape his future, brick by brick. As he walked through the grand entrance, he couldn't help but feel a sense of awe and determination. He was here to learn, to grow, and to build something meaningful out of his time at Elmwood.

The halls were bustling with activity as freshmen like him moved in, getting their first taste of independence. The smell of fresh paint mixed with the earthy scent of the old wood floors, creating a unique blend of the new and the old. As John made his way to his dorm, he passed by groups of students engaged in animated conversations, some about the latest scientific discoveries, others about the best place to get coffee on campus. It was a place alive with energy and possibility.

John's room was modest but comfortable, with a window that overlooked the sprawling green lawn where students gathered to study, relax, and socialize. He unpacked his belongings slowly, each item a piece of his past, now part of this new journey. The posters of his favorite bands, the books he'd read a dozen times, and the framed photo of his family - each one found its place in this new space.

As he settled in, John couldn't help but think about the students who had come before him, who had started their journeys in this very hall. They had built their futures here, one class, one friendship, one experience at a time. And now, it was his turn to add to the legacy of Elmwood Hall, to build his future, brick by brick.

Ramen Revolution

Highlights the initial chaos and excitement of dorm life

The dormitory was a flurry of activity from the moment John arrived. The narrow hallways were packed with students juggling boxes, laundry baskets, and the occasional armful of snacks. The air buzzed with the hum of conversation, laughter, and the unmistakable clatter of hastily assembled furniture. This was dorm life in all its chaotic glory - a whirlwind of new faces, cramped spaces and the exhilarating freedom of living away from home for the first time.

John quickly learned that survival in this new environment required a few key essentials: a sturdy pair of flip-flops for the communal showers, a reliable alarm clock, and, most importantly, a stash of instant ramen. Ramen noodles became the unofficial currency of the dorms, a culinary staple that transcended social circles and late-night cravings. It wasn't long before John's tiny dorm room became the epicenter of what he and his hall mates affectionately dubbed the "Ramen Revolution."

The first week was a blur of orientation events, awkward icebreakers, and navigating the maze of campus buildings. But at the end of each day, it was the communal experience of dorm life that brought everyone together. The smell of ramen - beef, chicken, and shrimp - wafted through the halls as students bonded over late-night cooking sessions in the shared kitchen. It was more than just a quick meal; it was a symbol of their shared experience, a unifying force in the midst of the madness.

John's dorm was a microcosm of college life, a place where chaos and excitement blended together in a way that felt both overwhelming and invigorating. There were the inevitable mishaps - like the time someone tried to microwave a metal bowl, or when the fire alarm went off at 3 a.m., sending everyone scrambling out into the cold night in their pajamas. But there were also moments of connection - impromptu study sessions in the hallway, movie nights crammed into someone's tiny room, and the endless debates about the best way to cook ramen (with an egg? add some hot sauce?).

Despite the chaos, or perhaps because of it, John found himself thriving in this new environment. The initial nervousness he felt about living with strangers quickly faded as he realized that everyone was in the same boat - excited, anxious, and eager to make the most of this new chapter in their lives. The dorm wasn't just a place to sleep; it was a community, a place where friendships were forged over shared experiences, and where every day brought something new.

The "Ramen Revolution" became a kind of tradition in John's dorm, a nightly ritual that brought everyone together no matter how stressful the day had been. As he stirred his latest concoction in a battered pot, surrounded by the familiar faces of his hall mates, John couldn't help but feel a sense of belonging. Dorm life was messy, loud, and unpredictable - but it was also full of energy and possibility. It was a place where memories were made, and where the foundations of lifelong friendships were laid, one bowl of ramen at a time.

Constellations Collide

Introduces John's roommates, Sam and Ben, and the forming of their friendship

John hadn't known what to expect when he first walked into his dorm room, but he certainly hadn't anticipated meeting Sam and Ben. The three of them were like different stars in the night sky, each with their own unique brightness, orbiting distinct paths. Yet, somehow, when their constellations collided in that small, shared space, a friendship was born that would shape their college experience.

Ben was the first to arrive. A tall, lanky guy with unruly curls and an easygoing smile, he immediately filled the room with his energy. Within minutes of meeting John, Ben had already started talking about his plans to join the campus radio station, his passion for indie music, and his mission to find the best pizza in town. He was the kind of person who could strike up a conversation with anyone, anywhere - a trait that both intrigued and intimidated John.

Then there was Sam. Quiet and reserved, Sam was the complete opposite of Ben. With neatly combed hair and glasses perched on the edge of his nose, he exuded a calm, studious vibe. When Sam walked in, he nodded politely at John and Ben, set his books on his desk, and began unpacking with meticulous care. Sam's passion was coding, and he had already secured a spot in the college's prestigious computer science program. Despite his introverted nature, there was intensity about Ben that drew people in, a quiet confidence that hinted at a depth of character beneath the surface.

At first, the three of them seemed like an odd mix. John, with his love of history and literature, Ben, the extroverted music lover, and Sam, the tech-savvy introvert. But as the days went by, they began to find common ground. Late-night conversations revealed shared interests and aspirations - John's fascination with ancient myths resonated with Ben's love of storytelling through music, and Sam's programming skills became an unexpected complement to their creative discussions.

One evening, as the sun dipped below the horizon, painting the sky with hues of orange and purple, the three of them found themselves sitting on the dorm room floor, surrounded by unpacked boxes and half-eaten snacks. It was in that moment, beneath the fading light, that the first seeds of their friendship were sown. Ben was strumming his guitar softly, humming a tune, while Sam was showing John a project he had been working on - a digital map of constellations, a hobby that combined his love for coding with his interest in astronomy.

"*You know,*" Ben said, pausing mid-chord, "*We're like constellations, the three of us. Separate stars, but when you connect the dots, we make something bigger.*"

John and Sam looked at him, surprised by the poetic insight from their usually light-hearted roommate. But it was true. They were different, yet their differences complemented each other in a way that made them stronger as a unit. The forming of their friendship felt like destiny, like their paths had crossed for a reason.

As the semester progressed, their bond only grew stronger. They balanced each other out - Ben's spontaneity pulling Sam out of his shell, Sam's analytical mind providing structure to Ben's creative chaos, and John acting as the glue that held them together, bridging their personalities with his thoughtful nature. Together, they navigated the ups and downs of freshman year, from acing exams to surviving the chaos of dorm life.

Their room became a sanctuary, a place where they could be themselves without judgment. Whether they were debating philosophy, collaborating on projects, or just hanging out, the connection they shared was undeniable. They were no longer just roommates - they were friends, a constellation of their own making, shining brightly against the vast, sometimes daunting, backdrop of college life.

The Labyrinth of Learning

Explores the initial challenges and discoveries in navigating college academics

The first few weeks of classes felt like being dropped into a vast, twisting labyrinth - a maze of lecture halls, textbooks, and endless assignments that seemed designed to confuse and challenge every student who dared to enter. For John, the transition from high school to college academics was a shock to the system. Gone were the familiar routines and the predictable flow of classes; in their place was a demanding schedule filled with rigorous coursework and the constant pressure to keep up.

John quickly realized that college was a different world, one where self-discipline and time management were no longer optional but essential. The professors were passionate and knowledgeable, but they didn't spoon-feed information the way high school teachers often did. Instead, they presented complex ideas and expected the students to dig deep, to question, to analyze, and to discover the answers for themselves. This was learning on a whole new level.

The first real challenge came in the form of his history class. John had always loved history - delving into the past, uncovering the stories that shaped the present - but this class was more intense than anything he had experienced before. The reading list was long and dense, filled with primary sources that required careful analysis. The essays demanded not just a regurgitation of facts but original thought, a deep engagement with the material that pushed John to think critically and creatively.

In the beginning, it was overwhelming. There were nights when John sat at his desk, staring at a blank screen, wondering how he would ever get through it all. The labyrinth seemed endless, with new challenges appearing at every turn. But as the days passed, John began to find his way. He developed new strategies for studying - color-coded notes, late-night study sessions with Sam and Ben, and regular visits to the library, where the quiet atmosphere helped him focus.

One of the biggest discoveries John made was the importance of asking for help. In high school, he had always been a good student, able to figure things out on his own. But college was different. The material was more complex, and the expectations were higher. It was during a particularly difficult week, when he was struggling with an essay on medieval history, that John finally swallowed his pride and sought out his professor during office hours. To his surprise, the professor was not only willing to help but seemed genuinely interested in guiding him through the challenges. That conversation was a turning point - it made John realizes that college wasn't just about getting good grades; it was about engaging with the material, learning from experts, and growing as a thinker.

John also discovered that the labyrinth of learning wasn't something he had to navigate alone. His classmates were facing the same challenges, and by working together, they could support each other through the rough patches. Study groups became a lifeline, a way to break down complex topics and share insights. Discussions that started in the classroom often spilled over into late-night debates in the dorms, where ideas were tested and refined. These collaborative efforts not only helped John keep up with his coursework but also deepened his understanding of the material.

Over time, what had initially seemed like an overwhelming maze began to feel more like a journey of discovery. Every twist and turn brought new insights, every challenge an opportunity to grow. John learned to embrace the uncertainty, to see the labyrinth not as a barrier but as a path to greater knowledge. The process was difficult, sometimes frustrating, but ultimately rewarding. Each small victory - whether it was finally understanding a difficult concept or receiving positive feedback on an essay - reinforced his confidence and fueled his desire to keep pushing forward.

By the end of the semester, John had not only survived his first round of college exams but had begun to thrive academically. The labyrinth of learning, with all its challenges and discoveries, had become a place where he could explore his passions, test his limits, and build a solid foundation for the years to come. The journey was far from over, but John knew that he had the tools and the determination to find his way, no matter how complex the path might become.

All – Nighters and Epiphanies

Captures the late – night study sessions, intellectual growth, and forming a sense of purpose

The campus was eerily quiet at 2 a.m., with only the soft hum of fluorescent lights and the distant rustle of trees breaking the stillness. While most students were fast asleep, John, Sam, and Ben were wide awake, huddled around their laptops in the common room. The dim light cast long shadows on their faces, reflecting the intense focus that had taken over their usual banter. These late-night study sessions, once a necessary evil, had become a ritual - moments where the pressures of looming deadlines gave way to unexpected bursts of creativity and insight.

It was during these all-nighters that John began to experience a different kind of learning, one that went beyond the confines of lectures and textbooks. The quiet hours of the night seemed to unlock something within him, a deeper level of thinking that was fueled by the solitude and the shared determination of his friends. The conversations that flowed in these hours were different too - more honest, more probing. They weren't just reviewing material for exams; they were exploring ideas, challenging each other's perspectives, and delving into topics that sparked their curiosity.

One night, as they sat surrounded by a sea of notes and empty coffee cups, the conversation turned to the purpose of their studies. "*Why are we doing this?*" Sam asked, more to himself than to anyone else. It wasn't a question of why they were cramming for a particular test or finishing an assignment, but a deeper inquiry into the reasons behind their education. What did they hope to achieve? What was the point of all this effort?

John had asked himself the same question more than once, especially during the toughest moments of his first semester. But in that moment, something clicked. He realized that the all-nighters weren't just about passing exams - they were about pushing his boundaries, testing his resilience, and discovering what truly mattered to him. The exhaustion he felt was not just a physical tiredness but a sign that he was stretching his mind in new ways, forcing himself to think critically and independently.

The epiphanies didn't always come in grand revelations. Sometimes, they were subtle, a quiet shift in perspective that emerged after hours of grappling with a difficult concept. Other times, they were more profound - like the night John finally understood the interconnectedness of the historical events he had been studying. It wasn't just about memorizing dates and facts; it was about seeing the bigger picture, understanding how the past shaped the present, and how his own journey was a part of that larger narrative.

These moments of intellectual growth were often accompanied by a growing sense of purpose. John began to see his education not just as a means to a degree but as a way to engage with the world, to contribute something meaningful. The late-night discussions with Sam and Ben played a crucial role in this development. Their different perspectives - Sam's creative approach to problem-solving, Ben's analytical precision - challenged John to think more deeply and to consider angles he hadn't before.

The all-nighters also strengthened their bond as friends. There was something about those shared experiences, the collective struggle against sleep and stress, which forged a deeper connection between them. They learned to rely on each other, to support one another when the workload seemed overwhelming, and to celebrate the small victories, like finally finishing a tough assignment or having a breakthrough idea.

As the semester progressed, the sense of purpose that had been slowly forming within John became more defined. He realized that his time at Elmwood was about more than just academic achievement. It was about discovering who he was, what he was passionate about, and how he could make a difference. The late-night study sessions were a crucible in which this purpose was forged, tempered by the challenges he faced and the insights he gained.

By the time finals week rolled around, John had pulled more all-nighters than he could count. But he didn't mind. He had come to embrace these late-night hours as opportunities for growth, moments when his mind was most alive, when the distractions of the day faded away, and all that remained was the pursuit of knowledge and understanding. Each all-nighter brought with it new challenges, but also new epiphanies - small spark of insight that illuminated his path forward, guiding him toward the person he was becoming.

Sophomore Year

Deepening Connections

Comfort in Chaos

Shows how the dorm room becomes a haven despite the surrounding craziness

As sophomore year began, the campus was alive with a familiar energy - busier classes, new responsibilities, and the constant hum of student life. The world outside their dorm room seemed to move at a frenetic pace, with deadlines looming, social events multiplying, and the pressure to succeed growing more intense. Yet, in the midst of this chaos, John, Sam, and Ben found an unexpected sanctuary: their dorm room.

The room itself was nothing special - a small, rectangular space with standard-issue furniture and walls that had seen their fair share of tape marks and thumbtack holes. But over the past year, it had evolved into something more, a place that reflected the personalities and the bond they had built. Posters of bands, movie quotes, and favorite books adorned the walls, while the shelves were filled with mementos from their first year together - ticket stubs from concerts, photos of late-night adventures, and souvenirs from impromptu road trips.

The room had a lived-in feel that was comforting in its familiarity. The clutter of textbooks, laptops, and half-empty coffee mugs was a testament to the hours they spent working, debating, and just being themselves. It wasn't perfectly tidy, but that was part of its charm. It was a space where they could let their guard down, where the expectations of the outside world didn't seem quite so daunting.

No matter how hectic the day had been, stepping into the dorm room felt like taking a deep breath. The noise of the campus faded into the background, replaced by the sounds of Ben strumming his guitar or Sam typing away on his laptop. The room had become a haven, a place where they could retreat from the demands of college life and find comfort in each other's company.

The craziness of sophomore year was inevitable. Classes were more challenging, and the stakes were higher. But within the four walls of their dorm room, John, Sam, and Ben found stability. It was a place where they could decompress after a tough day, venting about difficult professors or celebrating small victories. It was also where they could support each other through the ups and downs - whether that meant staying up late to help with a project, offering advice on a tough decision, or simply being there to listen.

The room wasn't just a physical space; it was the embodiment of their friendship. It was where they could be their true selves, without fear of judgment. When the world outside felt overwhelming, the dorm room provided a sense of control and calm. It was a place where they could recharge, regroup, and face the chaos with renewed energy.

As the year went on, the room became a hub for more than just the three of them. Friends from other dorms started to drop by more often, drawn by the warmth and camaraderie that seemed to fill the space. It wasn't uncommon to find a group of people sprawled across the floor, sharing stories, cracking jokes, and just enjoying each other's company. The dorm room had become more than just a haven for John, Sam, and Ben - it was a refuge for anyone who needed a break from the chaos of college life.

The comfort they found in the room wasn't just about escaping the outside world; it was about creating a space where they could grow together. The discussions they had within those walls - about their dreams, fears, and the future - deepened their connections and solidified their friendship. It was a place where ideas flowed freely, where they could challenge each other intellectually and support each other emotionally.

By the end of sophomore year, the dorm room had become a symbol of everything they had built together - a place of laughter, learning, and unshakeable bonds. It was where they had weathered the storms of college life and emerged stronger for it. In a world that often felt chaotic and unpredictable, the room provided a constant, a reminder that no matter what challenges lay ahead, they had each other and the comfort of their shared haven to return to.

The Poetry of Purpose

Highlights John's passion for literature and his academic journey

Sophomore year was a turning point for John, not just in his social life but in his academic journey as well. While freshman year had been about adjusting to college life and navigating the demands of his courses, this year marked the beginning of something deeper - a growing passion for literature that would shape his sense of purpose.

John had always loved reading. As a child, he would lose himself in books, transported to different worlds by the power of words. But it was during his sophomore year at Elmwood that his love for literature began to transform into something more - a passion, a calling, and perhaps even a future career.

It all started with a course on Romantic poetry. John had enrolled in it on a whim, curious about the poets whose works had influenced so many others. The professor, a dynamic and passionate scholar with an infectious enthusiasm for the subject, quickly became one of John's favorites. In this class, John discovered the depth and beauty of language in a way he hadn't before. The poems they studied weren't just words on a page; they were expressions of emotion, reflections on the human condition, and explorations of the natural world. John was captivated by how these poets could convey complex ideas and deep feelings with such elegance and precision.

As he delved deeper into the works of Wordsworth, Keats, and Shelley, John began to see literature not just as a subject to study but as a lens through which to understand life. The themes of love, loss, nature, and identity resonated with him, mirroring his own thoughts and experiences. The more he read, the more he realized that literature had the power to connect people across time and space, to speak to universal truths that were as relevant today as they were centuries ago.

The course ignited a fire in John. He found himself staying up late, not out of necessity but out of a genuine desire to explore the texts further. He started writing in his journal again, something he hadn't done since high school, jotting down thoughts and reflections inspired by the poetry he was reading. These late-night sessions became moments of introspection, where he could process the ideas he encountered in class and connect them to his own life.

John's passion for literature didn't go unnoticed. His professor, impressed by his insights and the quality of his essays, encouraged him to consider pursuing English as a major. The idea excited John. It felt like a natural progression, a way to channel his love for reading and writing into something more structured and meaningful. He began exploring the English department more closely, talking to other professors, attending literary events, and reading more widely outside of class. Each new discovery only deepened his commitment to the field.

But it wasn't just about academics for John. The literature he studied helped him make sense of his own journey. The characters he encountered, the stories they lived, and the emotions they experienced all contributed to his understanding of himself and his place in the world. He started to see his own life as part of a larger narrative, with its own themes, conflicts, and resolutions. This realization gave him a sense of purpose that had been missing before - a belief that his studies were not just a means to an end but a way to engage with the world on a deeper level.

John's newfound purpose also influenced his relationships. He began sharing his thoughts on literature with Sam and Ben, turning their late-night conversations into discussions about the books and poems that had moved him. While they didn't always share his enthusiasm for Romantic poetry, they appreciated the passion behind it and the way it had transformed their friend. These discussions strengthened their bond, adding another layer to the connection they had built over the past year.

As the semester progressed, John's academic journey took on a new direction. He declared English as his major, a decision that felt both exciting and daunting. There were moments of doubt, of course - worrying about the practicality of his choice, wondering if he was good enough to succeed in such a competitive field - but these were outweighed by the sense of fulfillment he found in his studies. For the first time, John felt like he was on the right path, one that aligned with his interests and values.

By the end of sophomore year, John had not only deepened his understanding of literature but had also found a purpose that extended beyond the classroom. The poetry he studied became a metaphor for his own journey - a journey of discovery, growth, and self-expression. It was in the verses of long-dead poets that John found his voice, a voice that would guide him through the rest of his college years and beyond.

Weekend Warriors

Showcases John's adventures with Ben, exploring the city and strengthening their bond

As sophomore year settled into its rhythm of classes, assignments, and study sessions, weekends became a treasured escape for John and Ben. While the demands of college life were relentless, the two friends found solace and excitement in their weekend adventures, which quickly became a tradition. These outings were more than just breaks from academic pressure; they were opportunities to explore the world beyond Elmwood Hall, deepen their friendship, and discover new aspects of them.

The city surrounding their college campus was a vibrant mix of history, culture, and modern life. It was a place where towering skyscrapers stood alongside cobblestone streets, where bustling markets coexisted with tranquil parks. For John and Ben, the city was an endless source of adventure, and each weekend, they set out with no particular plan other than to see where the day would take them.

One Saturday, they decided to hop on a bus and ride it to the end of the line, just to see where it would lead. They ended up in a part of the city neither of them had ever visited before - a neighborhood filled with quirky cafes, vintage shops, and street art. They spent hours wandering through narrow alleys, discovering hidden murals, and sampling pastries from a small bakery that had been there for decades. It was during this spontaneous exploration that John realized how much he appreciated Ben's sense of curiosity and his willingness to embrace the unknown. Their adventures were less about the destinations and more about the shared experience of discovery.

Another weekend, they ventured into the city's vibrant music scene. They stumbled upon a jazz club tucked away in a quiet street, where the sounds of saxophones and pianos filled the night. Neither of them had been particularly interested in jazz before, but the energy of the live performance was infectious. They found themselves tapping their feet and nodding along, immersed in the music and the atmosphere. The night ended with a long conversation over coffee, where they talked about everything from the improvisational nature of jazz to the challenges they were facing in school. These deep conversations, sparked by their shared experiences, brought them closer together and helped them understand each other on a new level.

Not all of their adventures were urban. On some weekends, they sought out nature, escaping the concrete jungle for the peace and quiet of nearby hiking trails and parks. One memorable trip took them to a sprawling nature reserve just outside the city. The hike was challenging, but the views from the top of the trail were worth every step. Standing there, looking out over a sea of trees with the city skyline in the distance, John felt a sense of clarity that was hard to find amid the chaos of college life. The physical exertion, combined with the beauty of the natural world, provided a much-needed reset. It was during these hikes that John and Ben often talked about their dreams and aspirations, the fresh air and open space encouraging a kind of honesty that was harder to reach in their dorm room.

Through these weekend escapades, John and Ben's friendship grew stronger. They learned to rely on each other, not just as study partners or roommates, but as true friends who could share both the joys and the struggles of life. Each adventure, whether it was a planned trip to a museum or a spontaneous exploration of a new neighborhood, added another layer to their bond. They discovered new interests together, from obscure genres of music to local history, and in doing so, they learned more about themselves and each other.

These weekends also provided a balance to the intensity of their academic lives. The city became their playground, a place where they could leave behind the stress of exams and papers, if only for a few hours, and just enjoy being young and free. Whether they were laughing over a failed attempt to navigate the subway system or sharing a quiet moment in a secluded park, these experiences reminded them of the importance of living fully, of making the most of their time at Elmwood.

As the year progressed, these adventures became an integral part of John's college experience. They were a reminder that life wasn't just about achieving goals and meeting deadlines; it was also about exploration, connection, and growth. The city, in all its complexity and vibrancy, became a backdrop for the stories they created together - stories that would become cherished memories long after their college days were over.

By the end of sophomore year, John and Ben had not only explored much of the city but had also explored new depths of their friendship. Their weekend adventures were a testament to the power of shared experiences, of stepping out of comfort zones and embracing the world with open minds and hearts. In the midst of the demands of college life, these moments of adventure and connection were what truly made their time at Elmwood special.

Unexpected Melodies

Introduces Ben's musical talent and the growing depth of their friendship

As sophomore year unfolded, John and Sam thought they knew all there was to know about Ben. He was the quiet one of the trio, the analytical mind who approached life with a calm, methodical demeanor. But as the semester progressed, Ben began to reveal a side of himself that neither John nor Sam had anticipated - one that brought a new dimension to their friendship and added unexpected melodies to their lives.

It started one evening when John returned to the dorm earlier than usual. As he approached their room, he heard the faint sound of music - soft, intricate notes that flowed together in a way that was both soothing and captivating. Curious, he pushed the door open and found Ben sitting on the edge of his bed, a guitar in hand, completely absorbed in the music he was creating.

John had seen the guitar in the corner of the room before, but Ben had never mentioned playing, and certainly never played in front of them. Now, watching Ben's fingers dance across the strings, John was struck by the contrast between the Ben he knew - the logical, often reserved friend - and the one he was seeing now, lost in the art of music. The melody was something John didn't recognize, an original piece that spoke volumes about the emotions Ben usually kept hidden behind his calm exterior.

When Ben finally noticed John, he stopped playing abruptly, almost embarrassed to have been caught. But John's expression was one of awe, not judgment. "*I didn't know you played,*" John said, breaking the silence.

Ben shrugged, setting the guitar down gently. "*It's just something I do to relax*," he replied, as if it were no big deal. But to John, it was a revelation.

Over the next few weeks, Ben's music became a more regular part of their lives. At first, he was hesitant to play in front of them, but with a bit of encouragement from John and Sam, he began to open up. It turned out that Ben had been playing guitar since he was a kid, a skill he had kept mostly to himself during his first year at Elmwood. Music was his way of processing the world, a creative outlet that balanced his otherwise logical and structured approach to life.

For John and Sam, Ben's music brought a new energy to their dorm room. The melodies that filled the space after a long day of classes were a welcome respite from the chaos of college life. Sometimes, Ben would play covers of songs they all knew, and they would sing along, laughing at their off-key attempts to harmonize. Other times, he would play his own compositions - beautiful, introspective pieces that spoke to the unspoken thoughts and emotions they all carried. Through these melodies, Ben communicated things he rarely expressed in words, and in doing so, deepened the bond between the three friends.

Their friendship grew in ways that John hadn't expected. The music created a shared experience that brought them closer together, adding another layer to their connection. It was during these impromptu jam sessions that John and Sam learned more about Ben's past - how his father had taught him to play guitar, how he had used music to cope with difficult times, and how it remained a constant in his life, even as everything else seemed to change.

One weekend, the three of them decided to take Ben's talent outside the dorm room. They found a small park on the edge of campus, where Ben brought his guitar and played under the open sky. The setting sun cast a warm glow over the scene as the music drifted through the air, attracting a few curious passersby who stopped to listen. It was one of those perfect moments where everything seemed to align - the music, the friendship, the simplicity of being together in that place. John realized that these were the moments that defined their college experience, not just the classes and exams, but the connections they were building, the memories they were creating.

Ben's music became a soundtrack to their sophomore year, a reminder that there was more to each of them than what was visible on the surface. It taught John and Sam to look beyond first impressions, to appreciate the hidden talents and passions that each of their friends possessed. And it deepened their friendship in ways that words alone could never have achieved.

By the end of the year, the unexpected melodies Ben had introduced into their lives had become an integral part of their story. His guitar was no longer just an object in the corner of the room; it was a symbol of the trust and openness that had grown between them. The music they shared wasn't just a hobby - it was a language that strengthened their bond, a way of communicating the things that were too complex for words. Through these shared experiences, John, Sam, and Ben forged a deeper connection, one that would carry them through the challenges and triumphs of the years to come.

Finding Our Voices

Represents the increasing confidence and self-expression of the characters

Sophomore year at Elmwood was a time of profound personal growth for John, Sam, and Ben. The initial adjustments of freshman year had given way to a deeper sense of self-awareness and confidence. As they navigated the challenges and opportunities of their second year, each of them began to find their voice - both literally and metaphorically - leading to a more authentic and self-assured expression of who they were.

For John, this newfound confidence was most evident in his approach to literature and academics. Having discovered a deep passion for poetry and writing, he began to take more risks with his work. No longer had content with merely meeting the expectations of his professors, John started experimenting with his writing style, exploring themes and forms that pushed the boundaries of his comfort zone. His poetry, once a private hobby, became a part of his academic work. He began sharing his pieces in workshops and literary events, receiving feedback and gaining validation from peers and professors alike. Each positive critique and encouraging comment bolstered his confidence, affirming that his voice was valuable and worth sharing.

Sam's journey of self-expression took a different path. While his creativity had always been evident in his artistic projects, he struggled with self-doubt and the fear of judgment. This year, Sam decided to confront these insecurities head-on. He began to take on more prominent roles in campus organizations, stepping out from behind the scenes to take leadership positions in creative projects and club events. His contributions were significant, from organizing art exhibitions to leading collaborative workshops. The more he engaged with his peers and took initiative, the more he realized that his ideas and leadership were not only appreciated but sought after. Sam's confidence grew as he saw the positive impact of his work and began to embrace his role as a creative force on campus.

Ben's path to self-expression was uniquely intertwined with his musical talent. His guitar playing, which had once been a private solace, became a way for him to connect more deeply with others. As he played his original compositions and covers in various settings - whether in the dorm, at park gatherings, or informal campus events - he found that his music resonated with people in unexpected ways. The vulnerability he expressed through his songs allowed him to connect with others on a more personal level. The positive responses he received from friends and strangers alike helped Ben shed his earlier reservations about sharing his art. He began to see his music not just as a hobby but as a powerful form of self-expression and communication.

As each friend found their voice, their connections with one another grew stronger. They began to support each other in new ways, celebrating their individual achievements and growth. John's confidence in his writing encouraged Sam to take bold steps with his art, while Sam's leadership and initiative inspired Ben to share more of his music. The trio's conversations became more profound and meaningful, reflecting the deeper understanding and respect they had for each other's journeys.

Their shared experiences also contributed to their individual growth. The late-night study sessions, spontaneous adventures, and heartfelt conversations fostered an environment where each of them felt safe to explore and express their true selves. The dorm room, once just a place of refuge, became a space of inspiration and creativity, where their voices could be heard and appreciated.

By the end of sophomore year, John, Sam, and Ben had each made significant strides in finding their voices. Their growing confidence and self-expression were evident not only in their personal achievements but also in the way they interacted with and supported each other. They had learned that self-expression was not just about making their voices heard but also about understanding and valuing the voices of those around them.

In finding their voices, John, Sam, and Ben had not only grown as individuals but had also deepened their friendship. Their shared experiences and mutual support had helped them navigate the complexities of college life and emerge more confident and self-assured. As they looked forward to the future, they knew that the journey of finding their voices was ongoing, but they were ready to face it together, with the strength and clarity they had gained throughout their sophomore year.

Junior Year

Facing Challenges

The Weight of Expectations

Addresses the pressure to choose a career path and the growing academic intensity

Junior year at Elmwood brought with it an undeniable shift in the atmosphere. The carefree explorations of the previous years were replaced by a more somber reality - time was slipping away, and the future was no longer an abstract concept but a looming presence that demanded attention. For John, Sam, and Ben, the pressure to choose a career path and navigate the increasing academic intensity became a heavy burden that tested their resilience and resolve.

As the year began, the trio found themselves caught in a whirlwind of expectations, both internal and external. The campus buzzed with talk of internships, graduate schools, and job prospects. Professors no longer emphasized the exploration of interests but instead focused on the practical application of knowledge and the importance of building a resume. The conversations in the dorm room shifted from late-night musings about life to anxious discussions about the future. What were they going to do after graduation? How would they turn their passions into viable careers? These questions hung over their heads like a dark cloud, intensifying the pressure they already felt.

John, who had always found solace in literature, now faced the daunting task of translating his love for words into a career. The romantic notion of becoming a writer or poet seemed increasingly impractical in the face of mounting student loans and the harsh realities of the job market. Advisors urged him to consider more "stable" paths, such as teaching or publishing, but John struggled with the idea of compromising his passion for security. The weight of these expectations began to take a toll on him, and for the first time, he found himself doubting his choices.

Sam, too, was feeling the strain. His artistic talents were undeniable, but the art world was notoriously competitive and unpredictable. While his heart was set on pursuing a career in graphic design or animation, the fear of failure loomed large. He started to question whether he should have chosen a more conventional path, one that guaranteed a steady income and job security. The pressure from his family, who worried about the practicality of an art career, only added to his stress. The once vibrant and confident Sam found himself second-guessing every decision, wondering if he was truly cut out for the path he had chosen.

Ben, with his analytical mind and musical talent, was torn between two worlds. On one hand, he excelled in his computer science courses and was practically guaranteed a lucrative job in the tech industry. On the other hand, his love for music was undeniable, and he couldn't shake the feeling that he was meant to do something more creative with his life. The pressure to make a decision weighed heavily on him - should he follow the safe, well-trodden path or take a risk on a passion that might not pay the bills? The uncertainty gnawed at him, and he began to withdraw, spending more time alone as he grappled with the conflicting desires within him.

The academic intensity of junior year only compounded these pressures. The coursework was more demanding than ever, with professors expecting not just completion but excellence. There was no room for error - grades now carried more weight, impacting their chances of getting into graduate programs or landing prestigious internships. The trio found themselves spending long hours in the library, fueled by coffee and a growing sense of dread. The pressure to excel, to prove themselves worthy of their chosen paths, was overwhelming.

As the year progressed, the weight of these expectations began to strain their friendships. The once-tight-knit trio found themselves snapping at each other over minor issues, their patience frayed by the constant stress. John, Sam, and Ben each retreated into their own worlds, consumed by their individual struggles. The shared sense of camaraderie that had defined their earlier years at Elmwood seemed to be slipping away, replaced by an unspoken tension that none of them knew how to address.

Despite the growing distance, there were moments of clarity that reminded them of the importance of their friendship. One night, after a particularly grueling week of exams and project deadlines, they found themselves back in their dorm room, exhausted and disheartened. The silence was heavy, but it was Ben who finally spoke up, admitting that he didn't have all the answers and that the pressure was getting to him. His honesty broke the tension, and soon, John and Sam were sharing their own fears and uncertainties. It was a cathartic moment, a reminder that they weren't alone in their struggles. The weight of expectations was still there, but at least they had each other to lean on.

By the end of junior year, the trio had faced some of their most significant challenges yet. The pressure to choose a career path and excel academically had tested their limits, forcing them to confront their fears and doubts head-on. While they hadn't found all the answers, they had gained a deeper understanding of themselves and each other. They realized that the journey was as important as the destination and that it was okay to not have everything figured out just yet.

The weight of expectations would continue to be a part of their lives, but they had learned that they didn't have to carry it alone. Together, they would face whatever challenges came their way, knowing that the support and understanding they had for one another would be their greatest strength as they moved forward.

A Constellation Dims

Deals with John's grief and the strain it puts on the friendship

Junior year had been a test of endurance for John, Sam, and Ben, but none of them could have anticipated the emotional storm that was about to engulf them. For John, what started as a semester full of pressure and academic challenges soon became a period marked by profound grief, a weight that would threaten to unravel not just his own sense of self, but also the tightly knit bond between the three friends.

It happened suddenly - a phone call in the middle of the night that shattered John's world. The news of his father's unexpected passing hit him like a tidal wave, leaving him adrift in a sea of sorrow and disbelief. The man who had been his greatest supporter, his mentor, and his role model was gone, leaving behind a void that John didn't know how to fill. The days that followed were a blur of funeral arrangements, condolences, and the mechanical motions of grief. John withdrew into himself, his once vibrant personality dimming under the weight of loss.

Sam and Ben, unsure of how to help, found themselves walking on eggshells around him. They wanted to be there for their friend, but they didn't know how. Every attempt to reach out seemed to fall flat - John either brushed them off with a hollow "I'm fine" or retreated further into his shell. The John they knew, the one who found solace in words and poetry, seemed to have lost his voice. His assignments went unfinished, his guitar collected dust, and he spent more and more time alone in his room, staring blankly at the walls or lost in restless sleep.

As John's grief deepened, so too did the strain on the friendship. The easy camaraderie they had once shared was replaced by awkward silences and unspoken tensions. Sam, usually the first to crack a joke or lighten the mood, felt helpless in the face of John's sadness. His attempts at humor felt inappropriate, even insensitive, and he worried that he might push John further away. Ben, more reserved by nature, found it difficult to navigate the emotional minefield that their dorm had become. He wanted to give John space, but he also feared that doing so would isolate him even more.

Their conversations became stilted, revolving around mundane topics that skirted the real issue at hand. The trio that had once been inseparable now felt fragmented, as if a vital piece of their constellation had dimmed, leaving them struggling to find their way in the dark. The strain was palpable, and each of them felt it, though none of them knew how to bridge the widening gap.

The turning point came one night when Ben, unable to bear the silence any longer, confronted John. It wasn't planned - it just happened, a burst of frustration and concern that had been building up for weeks. "John, you're shutting us out," Ben said, his voice tinged with both anger and desperation. "We know you're hurting, but we're your friends. We want to help, but we can't if you keep pushing us away."

John's reaction was immediate and raw. All the emotions he had been bottling up came spilling out in a torrent of words -

anger, sadness, guilt, and frustration. He lashed out at Ben, at Sam, at the world that had taken his father from him. The confrontation left them all shaken, but it was also a necessary release, a cathartic moment that laid bare the depth of John's grief and the strain it had put on their friendship.

In the aftermath of that night, something shifted. The confrontation, painful as it was, had broken the silence that had been suffocating them all. John, finally able to express some of the emotions he had been burying, began to let his friends back in. It wasn't easy - grief is a long and winding road, and there were still days when the weight of his loss felt unbearable. But slowly, with Sam and Ben by his side, John began to find his way through the darkness.

The healing process was slow and often painful. There were no quick fixes, no magic words that could take away the pain. But there was comfort in the small things - the shared meals, the quiet moments of understanding, the simple act of being together even when words failed. John's poetry, once a source of joy, became a way for him to process his grief, and he started writing again, slowly but surely. His friends, though they couldn't take away his pain, could at least bear witness to it, offering their support in whatever ways they could.

As the semester wore on, the bond between John, Sam, and Ben began to mend, albeit with new scars that marked their journey through this difficult time. The experience had changed them all - John had faced the darkest period of his life, and in doing so, had discovered a resilience he hadn't known he possessed. Sam and Ben had learned the limits of their ability to help, and the importance of simply being present, even when they didn't have the answers.

By the end of junior year, the constellation of their friendship, though dimmed by the weight of grief, had not been extinguished. Instead, it had been reshaped, its stars reconnected in new and unexpected ways. They had faced a challenge that could have torn them apart, but instead, it had brought them closer, deepening their understanding of each other and strengthening the bond that would carry them through whatever challenges lay ahead.

Lost in the Stacks

Represents John's feelings of doubt and confusion during the difficult academic year

Junior year at Elmwood was proving to be an obstacle course of challenges for John, one that he often found himself stumbling through rather than conquering. The academic pressure was intense, with the expectations higher than ever before. The demands of his coursework, coupled with the uncertainty of his future, left John feeling overwhelmed, and the library - once a sanctuary - became a symbol of his mounting doubts and confusion.

John had always found comfort in the stacks of Elmwood's library. The rows of books, filled with the wisdom of ages, had been a source of inspiration and solace throughout his college journey. But this year, the library took on a different, more oppressive character. Instead of finding clarity in the written word, John felt lost, as if the very stacks that had once guided him were now closing in, suffocating him under the weight of expectations and uncertainty.

The stress of choosing a career path weighed heavily on his mind. What had once seemed like a distant concern was now an urgent question that demanded answers he wasn't ready to give. John's passion for literature had always been his guiding light, but now that light flickered uncertainly, casting long shadows of doubt. Was pursuing a career in writing or academia a foolish dream in a world that seemed to value practicality and financial security over creativity and intellectual fulfillment? The pressure to make the "right" choice loomed large, and the options before him only deepened his confusion.

Each trip to the library, which had once been an eager pursuit of knowledge, now felt like a desperate search for something he couldn't quite grasp. He would wander the aisles, pulling books from the shelves, flipping through pages, but finding no answers. The once familiar texts felt alien, their words blurring together as his mind churned with anxiety. Research papers that had once excited him now seemed like insurmountable tasks, their deadlines approaching faster than he could manage. John found himself procrastinating, paralyzed by the fear of failure and the nagging thought that maybe, just maybe, he wasn't cut out for this after all.

The library's quiet, once a balm to his restless mind, now amplified his inner turmoil. The silence was no longer peaceful; it was oppressive, a constant reminder of the thoughts he couldn't escape. Even the sight of his peers, diligently working away at their own studies, only served to deepen his sense of isolation. How could they seem so sure, so focused, when he felt like he was drowning in a sea of uncertainty? John began to doubt his abilities, questioning whether he truly belonged at Elmwood, or if he was just an impostor pretending to have it all together.

His interactions with professors, too, became a source of stress. Their well-meaning advice about internships, graduate programs, and future careers only heightened his sense of confusion. The more they talked about the importance of making the right choices now, the more John felt the ground shifting beneath him. Every piece of advice seemed contradictory, pulling him in different directions and leaving him more uncertain than before. The weight of their expectations, combined with his own, was crushing.

The uncertainty wasn't limited to academics; it seeped into every corner of John's life. The grief he was still processing, the strain on his friendships, and the looming fear of the future all coalesced into a pervasive sense of being lost. He began to withdraw, spending more time alone, distancing himself from the friends who had once been his anchors. Even when he was with Sam and Ben, he felt disconnected, unable to articulate the depth of his confusion and doubt. The bond they shared, once so strong, now felt tenuous, as if it could snap under the strain at any moment.

There were days when John felt like giving up entirely - dropping out, leaving it all behind, escaping the relentless pressure. But even in his darkest moments, something kept him going, a flicker of the passion that had brought him to Elmwood in the first place. He couldn't completely abandon the love he had for literature, the joy he found in words, even when they seemed to elude him. This flicker, faint as it was, reminded him that there was still something worth fighting for, even if he couldn't see the path clearly yet.

By the end of the year, John hadn't fully emerged from the fog of doubt and confusion, but he had begun to understand that perhaps it was okay not to have all the answers. The journey through the stacks, though disorienting, had taught him something valuable: that uncertainty was a part of life, and that finding one's way was rarely a straightforward path. The key was to keep moving forward, even when the way seemed unclear.

The library, with its maze of books and quiet corners, had become a metaphor for John's internal journey - a labyrinth of doubt that he had to navigate on his own terms. And though he was still lost in the stacks, he knew now that the search itself was part of the process, and that sometimes, the act of searching was as important as the answers he hoped to find.

Discordant Notes

Shows the impact of Sam's personal struggles on the trio's dynamic

As junior year at Elmwood marched on, the pressures and challenges each of the trio faced began to surface in ways none of them had anticipated. Sam, who had always been the steady, analytical presence among them, found himself grappling with personal struggles that started to reverberate through the fabric of their friendship. The harmony that had defined their bond was now disrupted, as Sam's internal discord began to create fractures in their once unshakable dynamic.

For much of their time at Elmwood, Ben had been the one who could be counted on to keep a cool head, balancing John's creative intensity and Sam's playful exuberance with his own thoughtful approach to life. But beneath this calm exterior, Sam was wrestling with deep-seated issues that he had kept hidden from his friends. The pressure to excel in his computer science courses was mounting, and the expectations from both his family and himself to secure a high-paying job in the tech industry after graduation were suffocating. He felt torn between his passion for music, which brought him solace, and the practical demands of his academic pursuits.

Sam's struggles began to manifest in subtle but unmistakable ways. He became more withdrawn, spending long hours in the computer lab or locked away in his room, working on assignments that seemed to consume him. The time he once dedicated to playing music and jamming with John and Ben dwindled, and his guitar, once a constant companion, began to gather dust in the corner. When he did emerge from his self-imposed isolation, Sam was often irritable and short-tempered, a stark contrast to his usual composed demeanor.

The strain on the trio's dynamic was palpable. Conversations that had once flowed easily now felt stilted, with Sam's mood swings creating an undercurrent of tension. Ben, always quick to notice changes in their group, tried to draw Sam out, suggesting they go for a walk around campus or grab a coffee to talk. But Sam brushed off these offers, insisting he was fine, that he just had a lot on his plate. His evasiveness only deepened the concern that John and Ben felt, but they were unsure how to break through the wall Sam seemed to be building around himself.

The discord reached a peak during one of their rare group study sessions. What started as a discussion about a challenging assignment quickly devolved into an argument. Sam, frustrated with the direction of the conversation, snapped at John, accusing him of not taking things seriously enough. The harshness of his words stunned both John and Ben, who had never seen Sam so openly hostile. The room fell into an uncomfortable silence, and the once familiar and comforting presence of their friendship felt alien and strained.

John, who was already dealing with his own grief and academic doubts, took Sam's outburst to heart. He had always admired Sam's intellect and relied on his steady guidance, but now he felt as if he was losing another pillar of support. The growing distance between them only amplified John's feelings of isolation, making him question whether their friendship could withstand the pressures they were all facing.

Ben, on the other hand, tried to maintain a sense of normalcy, but even his boundless optimism couldn't mask the tension that had taken root. He missed the easy laughter and camaraderie they had shared, and he worried about what would happen if they couldn't find a way to reconnect. The trio, once in perfect harmony, now felt like a band playing out of tune, each member struggling to keep the rhythm as their own challenges pulled them in different directions.

The turning point came when Sam, after weeks of bottling up his emotions, finally broke down. It was late one night, after yet another argument, this time over something as trivial as which movie to watch. Sam's frustration and exhaustion spilled over, and he confessed to John and Ben the extent of the pressure he was under. He spoke of the fear that he wasn't good enough, that he was failing not just academically but as a friend, and the guilt he felt for shutting them out. His voice wavered as he admitted that he didn't know how to juggle his passions with the demands of his future, and that the weight of expectation was crushing him.

John and Ben listened in silence, the anger and frustration they had felt towards Sam melting away as they realized the depth of his struggle. They had been so caught up in their own challenges that they hadn't seen how much Sam was hurting. In that moment, the trio was reminded of the importance of their friendship, not just as a source of joy, but as a lifeline in times of need.

From that night forward, things began to change. The road to mending their bond wasn't easy - Sam still had to navigate his personal struggles, and there were times when the pressure threatened to overwhelm him. But now, instead of retreating into himself, Sam began to lean on John and Ben, accepting their support and understanding that he didn't have to face his challenges alone.

They found new ways to connect, whether it was through late-night talks that delved into their fears and hopes or impromptu music sessions where Ben would pick up his guitar and let the music soothe his troubled mind. The discordant notes that had once driven them apart became a part of their melody, adding depth and complexity to the friendship that had weathered so much.

By the end of the year, the trio had found their rhythm again, not in spite of Sam's struggles, but because of them. They had learned that true friendship wasn't about always being in harmony - it was about being there for each other, even when the music got tough. The discord that had threatened to pull them apart had, in the end, made their bond stronger, as they continued to face the challenges of life at Elmwood together.

The Fragile Tapestry

Highlights the threat to their friendship and the potential for everything to unravel

Friendship, like a delicate tapestry, is held together by countless threads of trust, understanding, and shared memories. At

Elmwood, the bonds that John, Sam, and Ben had painstakingly woven over the years were now at risk of unravelling. The pressures of junior year, compounded by personal challenges, introduced tensions that tested their relationship to its limits.

The trio, once inseparable, began to feel the strain of diverging paths and unspoken fears. John's grief over his father's passing cast a long shadow, leaving him withdrawn and distant. Sam, grappling with the fear of failure in his artistic pursuits, found himself doubting his place in the group. Meanwhile, Ben's internal conflict between his logical career path in computer science and his creative passion for music left him isolated, unsure of his role among his friends.

Misunderstandings grew as the trio, each consumed by their struggles, began to drift apart. Late-night conversations once filled with laughter and dreams turned into stilted exchanges. Efforts to bridge the gap often fell flat, as the fear of pushing too hard or saying the wrong thing kept them from addressing the growing rift. Each friend believed they were sparing the others from their burdens, unaware that their silence was fraying the very threads that bound them together.

The cracks in their tapestry became impossible to ignore after an emotional confrontation. Words that had been left unsaid finally came spilling out, raw and unfiltered. It was a painful but necessary moment that forced each of them to confront the truth: their friendship was on the brink of collapse, and saving it would require vulnerability and effort from all sides.

Despite the pain, the confrontation served as a catalyst for healing. Slowly, they began to open up, sharing their fears and insecurities. It wasn't easy - trust, once strained, is not easily repaired. But they chose to confront their struggles together, recognizing that their bond was worth fighting for. Through small acts of kindness, heartfelt conversations, and a renewed commitment to their friendship, they began to reweave their fragile tapestry.

The experience left their friendship changed but stronger. The threads of their bond, once frayed, were now reinforced with a deeper understanding of each other's vulnerabilities. They learned that the beauty of a tapestry lies not in its perfection, but in its resilience - the way it can endure unravelling and be rewoven, again and again.

Senior Year

The Enduring Echoes

Reclaiming the Light

Shows John's journey out of grief and the group's renewed support for each other

John's grief had cast a long shadow over their junior year, a darkness that threatened to pull the trio apart. Senior year, however, marked a shift - a gradual but determined journey toward healing and rediscovery. The light that had dimmed in John's life began to flicker once more, rekindled by the quiet persistence of his friends and the unshakable bond they shared.

The journey out of grief was neither quick nor linear. For John, it started with small steps - an unfinished poem finally revisited a reluctant laugh at one of Sam's bad jokes, and a late-night guitar session with Ben. Each moment, insignificant on its own, carried with it a promise of hope. The trio, too, began to find their rhythm again, their renewed support for each other becoming a guiding force. Sam's once-tense energy softened, his usual humor returning as he recognized that John's healing was a process they all shared. Ben, ever the quiet anchor, used his music to fill the silences that words couldn't reach.

It was during one of their regular evening walks through campus that John finally voiced what had been weighing on him. Under the pale glow of lampposts, he shared his struggles - the anger, the guilt, and the longing to move forward without leaving his father's memory behind. His words, raw and unfiltered, were met with unwavering understanding. "You're not alone in this," Sam said softly, a simple truth that carried the weight of their years of friendship.

Together, they began to rebuild what grief had fractured. Their dorm room, which had once felt suffocating, became a sanctuary again - a place of laughter, debates, and quiet moments of reflection. The trio found new ways to support each other, whether it was through late-night discussions, spontaneous trips into the city, or simply sitting together in comfortable silence. John's poetry, which had been his lifeline before, returned with newfound purpose - an outlet not just for his grief, but for the gratitude he felt toward the friends who had refused to let him drift away.

By the time senior year drew to a close, the light that had once seemed irretrievably lost was shining brightly again. John's journey out of grief had reshaped them all, teaching them that healing was not a solitary act but a shared effort, woven together by patience, love, and the quiet strength of friendship. As they stood on the cusp of graduation, the trio knew that whatever lay ahead, they had already overcome their darkest moments - together.

Harmony from Chaos

Represents Ben overcoming his challenges and finding his voice through music

Ben had always been the quiet one of the trio, his calm demeanor a stark contrast to Sam's exuberance and John's thoughtful intensity. But beneath his reserved exterior was a storm - a relentless conflict between his passion for music and the practical expectations of his future. Senior year would become the defining chapter of Ben's journey, where he found harmony amidst the chaos and, ultimately, his true voice.

The pressures of life after college loomed large as senior year began. The safety net of Elmwood's walls was fraying, and the world beyond was calling. For Ben, the choice between pursuing a stable career in computer science or following his deep-rooted love for music felt like an impossible one. His guitar, once a constant companion, had begun to gather dust again, a silent reflection of his growing uncertainty. Even Sam and John noticed the shift - the late-night jam sessions grew infrequent, and Ben's spark seemed to flicker.

It wasn't until a campus open-mic night that something changed. Sam, ever the instigator, signed Ben up without telling him. "You've been hiding your music for too long," Sam said when Ben found out, his voice firm but kind. "It's time to let the world hear it." Ben resisted at first, torn between fear of failure and the quiet longing to be heard. But as the night approached, something inside him stirred - a need to reclaim the part of himself that he had buried beneath expectations.

The small auditorium buzzed with energy as performers took the stage, one after another. Ben sat in the wings, his guitar clutched tightly in his hands, his heart pounding louder than the applause. When his name was called, he felt the familiar weight of doubt pressing down on him. But as he stepped into the spotlight, the chaos in his mind began to quiet. The audience blurred, and all that remained was the soft hum of the microphone and the strings beneath his fingertips.

Ben played an original piece - a melody he had written during one of his darkest moments, when the pressures of senior year had felt unbearable. The notes started softly, tentative at first, like a whisper searching for confidence. But as he played, the music grew bolder, his voice emerging not through words but through sound. Each chord was a release, a way of expressing the thoughts and emotions he had kept hidden for so long. The melody soared and dipped, weaving together the struggles he had faced and the hope that still lingered. By the time he struck the final note, the room was silent, every person holding their breath as if afraid to break the spell.

The eruption of applause was overwhelming, but it wasn't the clapping that mattered to Ben. It was the feeling of lightness that filled his chest, the sense that he had finally been honest with himself. Sam and John were on their feet in the front row, cheering louder than anyone, their pride unmistakable. For the first time, Ben felt seen - not as the quiet tech genius or the reliable friend, but as an artist, someone who had something real to share with the world.

From that night on, Ben's relationship with his music changed. He no longer saw it as a distraction from his responsibilities or an escape from reality - it was a part of who he was, as essential as breathing. Balancing his love for music with his practical career goals wasn't easy, but Ben stopped seeing it as a choice between two lives. He began to share his music more openly, performing at campus events and even recording a few original songs with Sam's help. His confidence grew with each performance, the chaos that had once defined his path now transformed into harmony.

Ben's journey taught all three of them a valuable lesson: that finding your voice doesn't mean silencing one part of yourself to amplify another. It's about embracing every piece of who you are, even the messy, uncertain parts, and creating something meaningful out of them. For Ben, music was no longer just a hobby or a passion - it was his voice, clear and unwavering, echoing far beyond the walls of Elmwood.

As graduation approached, the trio sat together on the campus lawn, the sun dipping below the horizon in hues of gold and purple. Ben strummed his guitar softly, a new melody weaving through the evening air. It was a song of reflection, of friendship, and of the journey they had taken together. "*You know*," Sam said with a grin, "*it sounds like you finally found your harmony*."

Ben smiled, his fingers dancing across the strings. "*Yeah*," he replied quietly, the music underscoring his words. "*I think I have*."

Graduation Echoes

Captures the bittersweet emotions of graduation and the end of their time at Elmwood

The final days at Elmwood were a blur of celebrations and goodbyes, a cacophony of emotions that resonated deeply within John, Sam, and Ben. Graduation, that long-anticipated event, had arrived, but with it came a bittersweet realization: their time at Elmwood was coming to an end. The campus, once a vast world of possibilities, now felt like a place of memories - some joyful, others marked by struggles - but all woven together into a tapestry of shared experiences that would stay with them forever.

For John, the prospect of leaving Elmwood was complicated. The halls, the dorm room, the library - all had been witnesses to his growth, his grief, and his triumphs. Walking through campus on the last day, he found himself reflecting on the journey that had begun so many years ago. His first nervous steps into Elmwood Hall, his late-night study sessions with Sam and Ben, and the poetry that had once been his solace now felt like distant echoes, each moment part of a larger, unfolding narrative. His grief, which had once threatened to define him, had transformed into something more - an understanding that healing is never linear, but rather, a continuous journey that carries us forward, no matter how uncertain the path may be.

Ben, too, felt the weight of the moment. He had come to Elmwood as a dreamer, unsure of his place in the world, but now, standing at the precipice of graduation, he had found not only his voice but his confidence. He had learned to navigate the chaos of expectations and pursue his passions without apology. Music, which had once been a quiet retreat, had become a cornerstone of his identity. But even as he looked forward to the future, there was a part of him that was reluctant to say goodbye to the place that had shaped him. The friendships, the late-night conversations, the laughter that had filled their dorm room - those were the things he would miss most. They were the echoes that would remain long after the campus was just a memory.

Sam, ever the quiet observer, struggled with a different kind of loss. Graduation meant leaving behind the friends who had been his anchors, the ones who had supported him through every challenge and triumph. But it also meant embracing a future filled with uncertainty - a future where the balance between practicality and passion would no longer be determined by the safe walls of Elmwood. Ben had found his voice, but now he had to find the courage to continue singing it in a world that would be far different from the one he had known. The thought of parting from Ben and John, the two people who had seen him at his best and his worst, filled him with both sadness and gratitude. Their friendship had been the steady rhythm in his life, and the idea of moving on was both exhilarating and heartbreaking.

The day of graduation arrived with the air thick with anticipation and nostalgia. The ceremony was a blur of faces - some smiling, others fighting back tears - but to John, Sam, and Ben, it felt as though the world had paused for a moment. The speeches, the diplomas, the handshakes - all were fleeting, like distant echoes fading into the background. What mattered most was the knowledge that, no matter where life would take them, the bond they shared would endure. They had grown together, stumbled together, and celebrated together. Elmwood had given them more than just an education - it had given them a foundation of friendship that would carry them forward.

As they stood on the steps of Elmwood Hall, their caps tossed high into the air; the echoes of their time at Elmwood began to settle into a quiet understanding. This was the end of one chapter, but it was also the beginning of another. They didn't know what the future held - what challenges or triumphs awaited them - but they knew they would face them together, even if from afar. The ties that had bound them for these four years were not so easily broken. They had each other's backs, no matter where life's journey would take them.

And as the sun began to set on their final day at Elmwood, the three friends shared one last moment together, each of them feeling the weight of the past and the excitement of the future. "*You know*," Sam said, looking at his friends with a grin, "*no matter what happens, we'll always have Elmwood*."

John and Ben nodded, their eyes filled with a shared understanding. Elmwood was more than just a place - it was a part of them, and it always would be. The echoes of their time there would follow them into the next chapter, a reminder of who they had been and who they were becoming.

Beyond the Brick Walls

Shows the characters venturing out into the world, carrying the lessons and memories of Elmwood

The towering spires of Elmwood Hall, once a symbol of challenge and opportunity, now stood as silent witnesses to the end of an era. For John, Sam, and Ben, walking away from the familiar brick walls was both a triumph and a farewell - a final step into the world beyond; armed with the lessons, memories, and friendships they had forged over the years. The campus, which had once seemed like an endless maze of possibilities, had shaped them into who they were. Now, it was time to take what they had learned and venture out into the unknown.

John stood at the gates of Elmwood, his thoughts a swirl of nostalgia and anticipation. He had arrived here as a wide-eyed freshman with an uncertain sense of direction, but now, he carried with him a purpose carved from his challenges and passions. His love for literature, once a quiet escape, had become the lens through which he viewed the world - a way to find meaning in the chaos of life. Elmwood had taught him not only how to think but how to feel deeply, how to see the beauty in every struggle. As he left the campus behind, he felt the weight of his father's memory not as a burden but as a legacy he would honor with every step he took.

Sam, ever the dreamer, couldn't help but pause and look back at the brick walls one last time. The campus had been his playground, a place where his creativity had found wings. He had discovered his voice here, not just through art and music but through the friendships that had carried him through his darkest moments. Now, the world beyond Elmwood felt vast and unpredictable, but Sam was ready. He had learned that chaos could be beautiful - that even when life felt uncertain, there was always a melody waiting to be heard. "*You ready for this?*" he asked, nudging Ben as they walked toward the road that led to their next chapter.

Ben nodded, his quiet confidence a reflection of how far he had come. For so long, he had wrestled with the tension between his practical ambitions and his creative passion. But Elmwood had taught him that he didn't have to choose - he could carry both parts of himself into the future. Music had become his anchor, and coding his canvas, two seemingly separate worlds that he now realized could coexist. "*Yeah,*" he said simply, his hand brushing against the guitar case slung over his shoulder. "*I think I am.*"

The three of them stopped at the edge of campus, where the brick walls gave way to open roads stretching toward the horizon. It was a quiet moment, one that didn't need words. They had walked these paths countless times over the years, often with laughter, sometimes with tears, but always together. Now, as they prepared to go their separate ways, there was no sadness - only gratitude for what Elmwood had given them.

John looked at his friends, his voice steady but soft. "*It's funny, isn't it? We spent so much time trying to figure out who we are, and now we're leaving with more questions than answers.*"

"*Yeah,*" Sam replied, a grin breaking across his face. "*But at least now we know we don't have to figure it all out alone.*"

Ben nodded, his gaze fixed on the horizon. "*Elmwood wasn't just about what we learned in class. It was about everything we experienced - the friendships, the failures, and the moments we didn't think we'd make it.*" He paused, his voice steady. "*We carry all of that with us.*"

The lessons they had learned at Elmwood were not confined to classrooms or textbooks. They were etched into their lives - lessons of resilience, of passion, of love, and loss. They had learned that success wasn't about having all the answers but about being brave enough to ask the right questions. They had discovered that friendship wasn't just about being there in the good times but about standing together through the hardest ones. And they had come to understand that the echoes of their time here would shape the people they were becoming.

With a final glance at the brick walls that had sheltered them for so long, they stepped forward - three friends carrying the weight of their shared past and the excitement of their separate futures. The road ahead was uncertain, full of challenges they couldn't yet see, but they were ready. Elmwood had given them the tools to face it: courage to embrace the unknown, creativity to find solutions, and a bond that would endure no matter how far apart they were.

As they walked away, the campus began to fade behind them, its echoes lingering like the final notes of a song. The brick walls had been their home, their refuge, their battleground - but the world beyond was waiting, and they carried its lessons with them. Wherever life would take them, Elmwood would always be a part of their story, a foundation upon which they would build the next chapters of their lives.

Elmwood Echoes On

A concluding chapter that emphasizes the lasting impact of their college experience and the enduring echoes of friendship

Years later, when the spires of Elmwood were no longer part of their daily view, its echoes still lingered - soft, steady, and enduring. For John, Sam, and Ben, Elmwood was not just a place they had once inhabited; it was a part of them, woven into the fabric of who they had become. Its lessons, its challenges, and the friendships they had formed there continued to shape their lives in ways both big and small.

John often found himself reflecting on those years when he taught his own students about poetry and literature. As a professor, he encouraged his class to see words not just as ink on paper but as vessels for truth, much like he had discovered during his own time at Elmwood. In the quiet moments before a lecture, he would sometimes think back to the late-night study sessions with Sam and Ben, the debates over coffee, and the first lines of poetry he'd dared to share. Elmwood had taught him to embrace both the beauty and uncertainty of life - a lesson he carried with him always.

For Ben, the echoes of Elmwood lived in the colors of his art and the melodies of his music. His creative pursuits, once fueled by the chaos of college life, had become a career that merged his passion for storytelling with design. Whether he was working on an animated short or composing music for a project, he always returned to the lessons of those years - the importance of trusting in the process, embracing imperfection, and finding beauty in the unexpected. He often joked that his best ideas came during quiet moments, like those spontaneous evenings spent laughing and dreaming with his two best friends.

Sam, ever the balance between logic and creativity, had carved out a path that reflected all parts of him. His career in technology was steady and fulfilling, but music remained his constant companion. He still played his guitar, its strings carrying not just notes but memories of Elmwood - of the first time he played for John and Ben, of the open-mic night where he discovered his voice, and of the quiet jams in their dorm room.

Whenever the world felt overwhelming, Sam returned to music, finding comfort in the echoes of his past and the friendships that had shaped him.

Though life had scattered them across different cities, their bond remained unshakable. Phone calls turned into visits, where laughter flowed as easily as it had in their college days. They reminisced about the "Ramen Revolution," the chaos of finals week, the confrontations that had tested their friendship, and the victories they had celebrated together. "*Remember when we thought graduation was the end?*" Sam would often say, grinning. "*Turns out it was just the beginning.*"

One summer, years after they had left Elmwood, the trio reunited on campus. The grounds were the same - brick walls standing tall, ivy climbing higher, and the cobblestone paths winding through familiar corners. Elmwood Hall, their anchor during those transformative years, loomed ahead as they walked through its archway, older now but still carrying the weight of their shared memories. Students bustled around them, laughing and racing to classes, much like they had once done. It was a bittersweet sight - proof that time moves on, but the essence of a place remains.

Standing in the middle of the courtyard, John looked at his friends and smiled. "*We've come full circle, haven't we?*"

Ben nodded, his guitar case slung over his shoulder, as always. "*Feels like we never really left.*"

Sam, his hands in his pockets, turned his gaze to the horizon. "*Elmwood isn't just here,*" he said quietly. "*It's in us - in every decision we make, every dream we chase, every challenge we face.*"

And he was right. Elmwood wasn't just brick and mortar, classrooms and dorm rooms; it was the friendships that had grown stronger with time, the lessons that had shaped their character, and the memories that echoed through their lives like a familiar song. The challenges they had faced there had taught them resilience. The dreams they had nurtured had become the foundation for their futures. The people they had been had led them to the people they were becoming.

As they left the campus that day, walking through the gates one more time, the echoes of Elmwood remained with them - not as a distant memory, but as a living presence. They carried it with them into their careers, their relationships, and their futures. It was in the way they supported others, in the risks they took, and in the moments they paused to remember that even in chaos, harmony could be found.

And so, Elmwood echoed on - not just in John, Sam, and Ben, but in every student who walked its halls, dreamed its dreams, and built friendships that could weather time. The place they had once called home had given them something eternal: the courage to face the world, the wisdom to embrace its uncertainties, and the strength to never walk alone.

Epilogue

Years later, the echoes of Elmwood Hall still resonated in the hearts of John, Sam, and Ben. Life had taken them on separate paths - John had become an accomplished writer, Sam a visionary designer, and Ben a celebrated musician - but the bond they had forged during those transformative years remained unbroken.

The lessons they learned within those ivy-clad walls had shaped not only their futures but also the way they approached life. Elmwood had taught them about resilience, the power of connection, and the enduring impact of friendship. It was more than a chapter in their lives; it was the foundation upon which they built their dreams.

On a crisp autumn evening, they found themselves back at Elmwood, standing once again in front of the hall that had been their sanctuary. Time had passed, but the memories were as vivid as ever - late-night talks, shared victories, and the quiet comfort of knowing they had each other.

As they walked through the familiar corridors, their laughter echoed once more, blending seamlessly with the voices of new generations. Elmwood had given them more than an education; it had given them a place in each other's stories.

And so, as they left the hall and stepped into the cool night, they carried the echoes of Elmwood with them, knowing that no matter where life led them, the friendship they had built there would always is a part of who they were.

By the Pen of Jirilin

The Elmwood Echoes is more than just a story; it is a reflection of the connections and moments that define who we are. As I penned this book, I sought to capture the intricacies of friendship, the resilience forged through challenges, and the bittersweet beauty of growth.

Through the lives of John, Sam, and Ben, I hoped to explore themes that resonate universally - the search for purpose, the power of shared experiences, and the lasting impact of genuine bonds. Their journey through Elmwood Hall mirrors the journeys we all take, where each step, each decision, and each relationship leaves an echo in our hearts.

Writing this book was not merely an act of storytelling but a deeply personal journey. I drew inspiration from my own experiences and the stories of those around me, weaving them into a tapestry of emotions, lessons, and unforgettable moments. My pen became a bridge, connecting my thoughts to the hearts of readers, creating a space where they too could see reflections of their own lives.

The magic of Elmwood lies not just in its halls but in the echoes of laughter, the weight of shared struggles, and the quiet moments of realization. It is my hope that **The Elmwood Echoes** reminds readers of the friendships they hold, and the memories that continue to shape them, long after the chapters of their own stories have turned.

www.ingramcontent.com/pod-product-compliance
Lightning Source LLC
LaVergne TN
LVHW090133160826
845673LV00017B/2460